20 BIG TRUCKS

in the Middle of the Street

MARK LEE

illustrated by KURT CYRUS

CANDLEWICK PRESS

One ice-cream truck selling everything sweet
Breaks down and blocks the middle of our street.

A mail truck stops, so now there are two.
Their drivers don't know what to do.

Watch out! Two trucks are in the way.
They stop a third truck carrying hay.

I start to count each truck I see.
First 1, then 2, and now there are 3.

A pickup truck is number 4.
A crane truck makes 5.
And here come more!

Two moving vans are 6 and 7.

Delivery trucks —
8, 9, 10, 11.

An officer blows his whistle.
Another waves her hands.

Truck 12 carries squealing pigs;
13 is piled with sand.

Cement is mixed in truck 14,
And 15 carries gasoline.

Truck 16 can tow a car;

17 pulls a kettle of tar.

Truck 18 has bread and rolls;
19 delivers meat.
A garbage truck makes 20 trucks . . .

Stuck in the middle of our street!

"Please look!" I say.
  "Can't you see?
The big crane truck
  is what you need!"

No one hears the
  words I say.
I'm too small.
  Just in the way.

So I stand in the street
    in the middle of the crowd
And say it again and say it loud:

"Look! There! Can't you see?
    The big crane truck is what you need!"

Then . . . "Oh!"
Then . . . "Yes!"
"We think that kid's idea
is best!"

The crane lifts
    the ice-cream truck up slow.
Now all the other
    trucks can go!

First one, then two,
    then three and four.
Five, then six,
    and more and more!

Till all the trucks are on their way,
Except for one that's here to stay. . . .

Just one truck on the side of my street.
An ice-cream truck selling everything sweet.

In memory of Diana Festa

M. L.

First edition 2013

Library of Congress Catalog Card Number 2012943654

ISBN 978-0-7636-5809-0

13 14 15 16 17 18 CCP 10 9 8 7 6 5 4 3 2 1

Printed in Shenzhen, Guangdong, China

This book was typeset in New Century Schoolbook.

Candlewick Press
99 Dover Street
Somerville, Massachusetts 02144

visit us at www.candlewick.com